# ANTHRACITE
# COUNTRY

# ANTHRACITE COUNTRY

POEMS BY

## JAY PARINI

RANDOM HOUSE
NEW YORK

"Coal Train" and "Near Aberdeen" first appeared in *The New Yorker.*
"Anthracite Country" first appeared in *Poetry.*
Other selections previously appeared in the following publications:
*The Agni Review, Atlantic Monthly, Georgia Review, The Hudson Review,*
*New Republic, Paris Review, Sewanee Review, Southern Review,* and *Yale Review.*

Library of Congress Cataloging in Publication Data
Parini, Jay.
Anthracite country.
Poems.
I. Title.
PS3566.A65A85   811'.54   81–10588
ISBN 0-394-52263-X   AACR2
ISBN 0-394-70454-1 (pbk.)

Manufactured in the United States of America
2  4  6  8  9  7  5  3
First Edition

FOR DEVON, *wife and closest reader*

The poets made all the words, and therefore language is the archives of history . . . a sort of tomb of the muses. For though the origin of most of our words is forgotten, each word was at first a stroke of genius, and obtained currency because for the moment it symbolized the world to the first speaker and to the hearer. The etymologist finds the deadest word to have been once a brilliant picture. Language is fossil poetry.

—Ralph Waldo Emerson

# Contents

# Amores

# This Reaping

# The Sabine Farm

*You spoke of Horace on his Sabine farm,*
*his lime-deep valley, hyacinth in bloom,*
*with holm oak forests shuffling in the breeze.*
*He loved the spring, the clover-laden grass*
*his herds would feed on, drizzle-sweetened hills.*
*He lived, well free of Rome, as if the world*
*were leafy and reposed, the weekly gossip*
*flowing from the courts Augustus kept:*
*a gabbling stream of anecdote, opinion,*
*downright lies. Through confident, warm years,*
*with kingly patrons tending to his needs,*
*he dug the furrows of his perfect odes.*

*I know a few of us would surely prize*
*that farm: soft fontanel of private earth*
*in which to plough the furrows of our verse,*
*to separate the tangled roots of speech,*
*possess the ground, the poet's measured tongue.*
*A few of us would love that greening world*
*with boundaries to walk and contemplate:*
*the pastures of desire, unweeded, blown*
*by riffles of blue wind; unforded brooks*
*of memory and dream; the icy cliffs*
*where waterfalls of purpose pour their vowels*
*through steady air, a music we could learn.*

*My friend, we follow in the Roman colter's*
*wake in our own ways, not really farmers,*
*but poachers on the farm Maecenas granted.*
*Now weekly gossip flows along the wires*
*from Boston to Vermont; the capital's*
*alive, but Caesars in their private jets*
*want nothing of us now. The mailman comes*
*with letters to aggrieve us, forms to fill.*
*I pay my debts, as you do, with a shrug*
*and turn to cultivate the ground, protected*
*by the barbed-wire fencing of our prose.*
*Unpatronized, we groom this inward land.*

# Anthracite Country

# Beginning the World

The crossing from sleep to waking
was easy those early winter mornings
when the snow fell dumb and bright as stars.

My mother packed me to the nose
in scarves; she tied a hat to my head
and sent me stumbling in boots through hills of snow.

The way was a desert of white,
dunes whirling in the street where cars
lay buried, humped and sleeping like camels.

And I loved that whiteness,
the unyielding blankness of it all
that left me alone with the whole world unimagined.

Today, marooned by decades
and distance from those days and winters,
I close my eyes to begin the world again.

# Walking the Trestle

They are all behind you, grinning,
with their eyes like dollars, their shouts
of *dare you, dare you, dare you*
broken by the wind. You squint ahead
where the rusty trestle wavers into sky
like a pirate's plank. And sun shines
darkly on the Susquehanna, forty feet
below. You stretch your arms
to the sides of space and walk
like a groom down that bare aisle.
Out in the middle, you turn to wave
and see their faces breaking like bubbles,
the waves beneath you flashing coins,
and all around you, chittering cables,
birds, and the bright air clapping.

# Playing in the Mines

Never go down there, fathers told you,
over and over. The hexing cross
nailed onto the door read DANGER, DANGER.
But playing in the mines once every summer,
you ignored the warnings. The door
swung easier than you wished; the sunlight
followed you down the shaft a decent way.
No one behind you, not looking back,
you followed the sooty smell of coal dust,
close damp walls with a thousand facets,
the vaulted ceiling with a crust of bats,
till the tunnel narrowed, and you came
to a point where the playing stopped.
You heard old voices pleading in the rocks;
they were all your fathers, longing to fix you
under their gaze and to go back with you.
But you said to them NEVER, NEVER,
as a chilly bile washed round your ankles.
You stood there wailing your own black fear.

# 1913

*"Guarda, Ida, la còsta!"*
She imagined, as she had for weeks,
a dun shore breaking through the fog,
a stand of larkspur, houses
on the curling bay.

As wind broke over the gunwales,
a fine low humming.

It was sudden when she came
to rest, the *Santa Vincenta*, thudding
into dock. The tar-faced lackeys
lowered the chains, seals
popped open, and the ship disgorged
its spindly crates, dark trunks
and children with their weepy frowns.
There were goats and chickens,
litters and a score of coffins
on the wharf at once.

Cold, wet, standing by herself
in the lines of custom
under some grey dome, rain falling
through the broken glass above her,
she could think of nothing
but the hills she knew:
the copper grasses, olives
dropping in the dirt, furze
with its yellow tongues of flower.

# The Missionary Visits
# Our Church in Scranton

He came to us every other summer
from the jungles of Brazil,
his gabardine suit gone shiny in the knees
from so much praying.

He came on the hottest Sunday, mid-July,
holding up a spear before our eyes,
the very instrument, we were told,
which impaled a brace of his Baptist colleagues.

The congregation wheezed in unison,
waiting for the slides: the savage women
dandling their breasts on tawny knees,
the men with painted buttocks
dancing in a ring.

The congregation loosened their collars,
mopped their brows, all praying
that the Lord would intervene.

Always, at the end, one saw the chapel:
its white-baked walls, the circle of women
in makeshift bras, the men in shirts.

They were said to be singing a song of Zion.
They were said to be wishing us well in Scranton.

# Heartland Lake:
# Bible Camp, 1961

It shivers in its skin,
an obsidian plaque of light,
blue squint of water
cupped among the pine, bright
ring of everything hard and lasting.
We come as children
of the heart's disease,
thick-tongued, repentant,
pushing with bare knees
through huckleberry, vetch,
red thickets of despair,
the loam of memory dragging
our heels, the buckthorn
flinging its accusations.
Crowns of midges
buzz our heads as we kneel
down, our prayers small
vapors in the evening air,
the lake's eye bloody
in the falling sun.
Hands linked and singing,
we gather in a ring,
the dead moon rising
in a mist of pink, all
hanging on the verge of
what we need: a sign
or wonder, something
we can name, the visionary's
blue-tipped flame, a run
of comets in the darkling sky.
Bullfrogs belly from a mud-
wet bank their pulsing
stanzas, crickets bleeping
in the night-rinsed grass
as we sing one chorus
of "The Shepherd's Brow"
and some weep greatly
for the world's black heart

that will never soften
nor admit these longings
nor accept this joy.

# The Miner's Wake

*in memoriam: E.P.*

The small ones squirmed in suits and dresses,
wrapped their rosaries round the chair legs,
tapped the walls with squeaky shoes.

But their widowed mother, at thirty-four,
had mastered every pose of mourning,
plodding the sadness like an ox through mud.

Her mind ran well ahead of her heart,
making calculations of the years without him
that stretched before her like a humid summer.

The walnut coffin honeyed in sunlight;
calla lilies bloomed over silk and satin.
Nuns cried heaven into their hands

while I, a nephew with my lesser grief,
sat by a window, watching pigeons
settle onto slag like summer snow.

# Coal Train

Three times a night it woke you
in middle summer, the Erie Lackawanna,
running to the north on thin, loud rails.
You could feel it coming a long way off:
at first, a tremble in your belly,
a wire trilling in your veins, then diesel
rising to a froth beneath your skin.
You could see the cowcatcher,
wide as a mouth and eating ties,
the headlight blowing a dust of flies.
There was no way to stop it.
You lay there, fastened to the tracks
and waiting, breathing like a bull,
your fingers lit at the tips like matches.
You waited for the thunder of wheel and bone,
the axles sparking, fire in your spine.
Each passing was a kind of death,
the whistle dwindling to a ghost in air,
the engine losing itself in trees.
In a while, your heart was the loudest thing,
your bed was a pool of night.

# Spring in the New World

Night rinsed the grasses.
Black geese scissored
through a waxing moon,
the stubble in the cornfields
wet and blazing. Down
beside the toolshed's
peeling clapboard, junk cars
burned, old hoops and fenders
heaped against the wall.
The children of the block
would go together to the swollen
river. Mayday. Nothing
in the world could stop
their march among the weeds:
mullein and yarrow, milkweed
pods, when everything
was drenched. The Susquehanna
slobbered at the shore.
The children flowed,
a tributary stream of blood
and skin encountering the air
and icy water. Children
washed the winter from their
bodies, floating on their
backs beneath the rail bridge
arching overhead, the iron
rainbow of a diesel world.

# Carnival Summer

The hog-bellied farmer hit the gong,
his fat arms wheeling; women in the crowd
leaned back and sighed. An epileptic
child fell down and shuddered.
Kids in wheels of chromium and steel
tore round the track.
An aisle of mirrors flickered
all the looks of sad-eyed women
waiting to be asked, of boys with thunder
in their pockets, combs and magazines.

I watched a dancer in the darkest tent,
her face like fudge, white cotton hair.
She put a record on the small machine
and let the music disarrange her limbs.
She threw her red silk panties into air
and let the farmers touch her with their chins.
And then she called me, "You there
with the hat, come have a look!" I put
a dollar on the stage and left,
the laughter ripping in my head all night,
her wide hips roiling in the canvas dark.

# Tanya

One day after school
I was running the tracks
back into the country
in early spring, sunlight
glazing the chips of coal,
old bottles and beer cans
shoaling the sides. I ran
for miles, stripped
to the belly, dogwood
odors in the air like song.

When I stopped for breath
I saw there were women
bending in the ferns.
They spoke in Polish,
their scarlet dresses
scraping the ground
as they combed for mushrooms,
plucking from the grass
blond spongy heads
and filling their pouches.

But the youngest one
danced to herself in silence.
She was blond as sunlight
blowing in the pines.
I whispered to her . . . *Tanya*.
She came when the others
moved away, and she gave me
mushrooms, touching my cheek.
I kissed her forehead:
it was damp and burning.

I found myself sprinting
the whole way home
with her bag of mushrooms.
The blue sky rang
like an anvil stung
with birds, as I ran

for a thousand miles to Poland
and further east, to see her
dancing, her red skirt
wheeled in the Slavic sun.

# Snake Hill

The dirt road rose abruptly through a wood
just west of Scranton, strewn by rusty wire,
abandoned chassis, bottles, bits of food.

We used to go there with our girls, those nights
in summer when the air like cellophane
stuck to your skin, scaling the frenzied heights

of teenage lust. The pebbles broke like sparks
beneath our tires; we raised an oily dust.
The headlights flickered skunk-eyes in the dark.

That way along the hill's illumined crown
was Jacob's ladder into heaven; cars
of lovers, angel-bright, drove up and down.

There was a quarry at the top, one strip
worked out, its cold jaws open, empty-mouthed.
A dozen cars could park there, hip to hip.

There I took Sally Jarvis, though we sat
for six hours talking politics. I was
Republican, and she was Democrat.

We talked our way through passion, holding hands;
the moon, gone egg-yolk yellow in the sky,
tugged firmly at our adolescent glands.

I kissed her once or twice, far too polite
to make a rude suggestion, while the stars
burned separately, hard as anthracite.

The city was a distant, pinkish yawn
behind our backs as we leant head to head.
The dead-end quarry held us there till dawn.

# Columbus in Downtown Scranton

His eagle forehead crowned with pigeons,
he stands majestic in Courthouse Square,
a long eye fastened to the farthest hills,
and a finger pointing westward.
He was our first hero,
claiming a round and palpable world.

We had a teacher in the seventh grade,
a Miss Krupinsky, and she liked to tell
how king after king refused him
ships and money, *but he persevered.*
She hung his portrait on the wall
up front between Ike and Nixon.

Now he soars above us, arching
a knuckle over those beneath him
in their daily round: the beer-bellied
men with black cigars, the ancient ladies,
the policemen dozing in armored cars,
the teenage gang-boys gunning their bikes.

# Working the Face

On his belly with a coal pick
mining underground:
the pay was better for one man
working the face.
Only one at a time could get
so close, his nose
to the anthracite, funneling
light from a helmet, chipping,
with his eyes like points of fire.
He worked, a taproot
tunneling inward, layer
by layer, digging
in a world of shadows,
thick as a slug against the floor,
dark all day long.
Wherever he turned, the facets
showered a million stars.
He was prince of darkness,
stalking the village at 6 P.M.,
having been to the end of it,
core and pith
of the world's rock belly.

# The Lackawanna at Dusk

Here is a river lost to nature,
running in its dead canal
across the county, scumming its banks.
I lean out over the water,
poking my head through rusty lace
of the old rail bridge and blowing
my spits out into the swill.
A slow wind ushers the homely smell
around my head; I breathe its fumes.
In whirlpool eddies, odds
of garbage and poisoned fish
inherit the last red hour of light.
A ripe moon cobbles the waters.
Mounds of culm burn softly into night.

# Anthracite Country

The culm dump burns all night,
unnaturally blue, and well below heaven.
It smolders like moments almost forgotten,
the time when you said what you meant
too plainly and ruined your chance of love.

Refusing to dwindle, fed from within
like men rejected for nothing specific,
it lingers at the edge of town, unwatched
by anyone living near. The smell now
passes for nature. It would be missed.

Rich earth-wound, glimmering
rubble of an age when men
dug marrow from the land's dark spine,
it resists all healing.
Its luminous hump cries comfortable pain.

# Groundings:
# A Sequence

# The Rain School

I entered the rain school, mud and water—
where the words were almost sensings, splashed,
a sibilant cool stream—that summer
when the river's tongue grew thick and frothy
and the town afraid. The city fathers

gathered on the banks to watch it brim,
the Lackawanna feeding on itself.
The women closed in circles of despair,
imagining a planet dowsed and drowned,
a biblical demise. I gorged my ankles,

trekking by myself, a slop of steps
through silt that left no open-ended vowels,
a vanished printing. Wading, I was
far out, plunging in the mud,
the subsoil gouged and healing underneath.

# The Salt Lick

I found this jawbone relic of a deer.
The brook beside it gargled in the strait,
a narrow rapids, something of a ford.
White foam and algae lathered where the hinge
once bit for apples, licked for salt.

An arrow in its side, perhaps a bullet,
this is where it fell. The hunter
never followed in its tracks. And here
it settled into hard, cold sleep
and lost the will to stumble farther on.

One night I dug its body to restore it:
set the hazel jelly of its gaze,
refilled the silken pouches of its lungs
and stretched new hide. It wakened into air!
I watched it loping to its thicket lair.

# Perch

I fished in a green pond fat with perch.
Their yellow bodies lit the water,
flashed like bulbs and disappeared below.
The sultry water lipped the banks
of fiddleheads and moss; the blond reeds swayed.

I waited for a sudden twinge of life,
gold muscle on a string,
then jerked to hook it firmly in the jaw.
Its razor tailfin plashed the mirror,
broke the glazed image of my face.

I studied it: the bright, findrinny scales,
soft blastings of its heart, a ventral shudder,
bare teeth needling the air,
its silent vowel opened into death.
The droplets of its eyes were slow to dry.

# Learning to Swim

That summer in Tunkhannuk the cold stream
barked, dogs herding over stones. Behind me,
wading with a switch of willow in your hand,
you drove me out: large father
with your balding, sun-ripe head, quicksilver

smiles. I wavered over pebbles,
small, white curds, and listened into fear:
the falls that sheared the stream close by,
the gargle and the basalt boom.
"It's safe," you said. "Now go ahead and swim."

I let it go, dry-throated, lunging.
Currents swaddled me from every side,
my vision reeling through the upturned sky.
Half dazed and flailing in a whelm of cries,
I felt your big hand father me ashore.

# After the Dance at Nugent Lake

In their blue-bright jeans, slim-hipped,
the young wade out among the cars;
the dance is over. Down beside the lake's
late-summer smell of motor oil
and mud, their world is wheeling.

Throbbing locusts cover up the clash
of teeth and tongue, the zippers split
like surgical incisions, the slapping thighs.
Old stars pop open, peepers in the sky.
The fish mouths rise and gargle at the moon.

I stand behind the hedges, learning
hard. One couple turns their bodies
in the sand, laid on this pyre.
The moonface gleams, white buttocks flare.
A comet whispers through the sky and dies.

# A Girl in June

The yellow mud-flowers sputtered in the sun
as she bent down, a lady in her smock
of white and gold, gold-plaited hair
dropped forward like a falls,
the wrists of water dangled from a crest.

I didn't know her by her name but watched
how in a soft, abstracted silence
she would pluck the bloom off salty grass,
an early summer harvest delicately
drawn from stubble near a marsh.

The yellow petals glimmered in a pail,
a blaze of lightning caught and coiled.
She sat beside them, taking to herself
the brightness gathered from a random ground.
She didn't know what brightness she had tamed.

# Berry-Picking

In July the huckleberries ripened.
Bushes swarmed with honeybees and wasps.
We worked in pairs, first scouting
from a bluff for clustered crops. I filled
my pail, my fingers gashed and bloody with the juice.

In corners where the rest would never guess
we'd gone, I gave you fistfuls,
berries from my hoard. Our stomachs swelled;
the black juice stained the innocence of smiles.
We lay on moss-banks thick as suede.

I told you that your lips were Beaujolais,
unsure of what I meant. You stroked my chin
and swore to wear the letters of my school.
Our friends would never see us as we were:
my hands, the rose-blown color of your teats.

# New Water

Spring hill of the world,
old mound of clay, of culm and coal chips
greening underfoot: I climbed
to listen when the ice was melting,
blue ice broken by a child's foot.

And water fizzled in the grass—
a gargle underground raised up and soaking
through the brindled turf.
I put my ear down,
listened to repeat the stammered sound:

the consonants like wood or reedy fiber
filtering the stream,
cold vowels poured through sleeves
of straw or straits of gravel;
clear words rising rinsed the tongue.

# Her Dying

Her pain began with sudden summer rain,
a splatter in the leaves, the roof-slates
ticking, tar smells risen from the oily road.
The ashen water filled the gutters,
clogged the drains with garbage and debris.

Her pain began with lightning in the hills,
the inward shudder of a small distress;
my grandma, latching windows in the hallway,
watched the sky, its sickly shimmer
through the limbs of shagbark hickory and oak.

Bad water sluiced the channels of her veins
and settled in her bowels. I saw her
founder in the wash of hours: black rains
that memorized her heart aloud—
and fell and fell.

# The Sea Lily

I found it on a culm bank near Old Forge:
the fossil of an ancient crawler
printed firmly in a slab of coal.
I took it home, the image of its delicate
horned shell and pincer-claws.

That summer in my bedroom, late one night,
I woke: a green moon eerily aflame
had caught the fossil in its funnel-light.
The creature shone, its eyes
were globed fruit swaying on their stems.

Last night I saw it shining in a dream,
the cilia on fire. Unnerved, I fossicked
in a book to find its name,
a miner in the word-bank, digger
in the tongue's lost gleaming quarry.

# Amores

# Morning on the Island

Such a palaver of sunlight!
It was morning on the island in summer.
A pierce of sea gulls woke me
as the wind blew up from wide-flung windows
where she stood, Corinna, naked,
gazing at the sea below.

The sun poured over her shoulder,
and her hair played loose with shadows.
Moisture sweetened her back;
she was cool as marble.

I gathered her body with my glance:
the angle of her breasts,
her legs as slender as a crane's.

She kept so still,
the silent music of her moved me,
Corinna,
idling in the sun like dust.

# Amores (after Ovid)

An afternoon in sultry summer.
After swimming, I slept on the long divan,
dreaming of a tall brown girl.

Nearby, a din of waves
blasted in the jaws of rocks.
The green sea wrestled with itself
like a muscular beast in the white sun.

A tinkle of glasses woke me: Corinna!
She entered with fruit and wine.
I remember the motion of her hair
like seaweed across her shoulders.

Her dress: a green garment.
She wore it after swimming.
It pressed to the hollows of her body
and was beautiful as skin.

I tugged at the fringe, politely.
She poured out wine to drink.
"Shy thing," I whispered.

She held the silence with her breath,
her eyes to the floor, pretending,
then smiling: a self-betrayal.

In a moment she was naked.
I pulled her down beside me,
lively, shaking like an eel—
loose-limbed and slippery-skinned.
She wriggled in my arms at play.

When I kissed her closer
she was wet beneath me and wide as the sea.

I could think of nothing but the sun,
how it warmed my spine as
I hugged her, shuddering all white light,
white thighs. Need more be said

but that we slept as if
the world had died together with that day?

These afternoons are rare.

# In the Meadow

Old Guernseys hover in the sun,
their brown sides hung from nape
to tailbone, a two-pole tent,
their legs like switches. Walking

in the meadow, we step over dung:
the dry flat discs, some wet with midges.
Daisies sputter in the heat
as we lie down, the milkweed crushing

beneath our backs its creamy stems.
We shiver in our skins.
Who looks beyond us, tangled, feeling
for what we are, looks too far.

# Seasons of the Skin

The beginning was hills, moss-covered stones,
October flowers. I climbed all day,
those damp beginnings. I felt
your arms like roots around me, love
like burdocks clinging to my legs;
the trees cried nothing but wind.

Winter was a crop of bones.
I remember your valley rimed with frost,
the slippery ledges, branches under snow.
I saw that your eyes were ponds of love
locked over with ice. I pecked
for a season into that gaze.

The spring was running. Icicles,
glazed by sunlight, narrowed to a drip,
and the moon shot awkward glances.
A nub of crocus started from your belly;
there was water spinning over stones.
I listened in the green-leaved wind.

Then a jay flipped over the pines,
a blue tail flashing. Sunlight
sharpened its edges on the rocks,
and feathery bracken softened your body.
I drew upon you in the heated grass
to see that your eyes were open water.

# Swimming in Late September

We listen:
the hush of apples falling through a dark,
the crackling of pines.
A slow wind circles the pond
like an ancient bird with leathery wings.

I float, my belly to the moon,
lifting my toes through cold, black water.
You brush against me, fanning your hair,
so close we are touching head to foot.

Frog-eyes sparkle in the ferns
as if they wonder
who would be swimming in late September.
Already the crickets have lost their wings;
the woods are brittle yellow.

But we go on swimming, swimming.
It is part of our love.
We give off rings of chilly waves
from one still center. Tonight
there is nothing but skin between us:
the rest is water.

# Fluting the Sea

While she beat the bread
into loaves, I crouched
by the sea with a flute in hand.

Below me, the cobalt surf
stung cliff and shingle.

Cormorants gathered on a bank
of water, mewing, grazing.

I blew thin notes
through the salt-green air
and thought how Orpheus

first drew tears
from the eyes of Furies
for hard love's sake.

I, too, would have challenged
the company of death
for your love, Corinna.

But our days had tangled
like a fisher's net
when the haul is in.

"Will you always love me?"
"Can you mean what you say?"

Impossible words like waves
split over our days.

# Waking on My Own

A blue light settles on the snow
like a Chinese bird with chalky wings.
I lean to the window at seven-thirty,
watching a blackbird peck at ice.

I pull my socks on, rub my nose—
thinking how she used to snug behind me,
snaking her legs around my belly,
breathing summer into my back.

A rope of wind snaps through the window,
stinging my chest. I blow my fingers
and look outside. My neighbor is busy;
his chain saw dips through buttery pine.

I putter by the sink. A cup and spoon
from yesterday's breakfast still need washing.
My pot of coffee is three days old.
I wonder how she lives in California.

"What a storm in Vermont!" my letter runs.
"I walked for an hour into the blizzard
to get some milk. The plumbing froze.
I am starting a poem with you in mind."

Now empty pages gather on my desk.
At night, I haven't a life to dream.
I blow on the window and write her name
to see how the letters weep and blear.

# Winter of the Dog

Blue winds harrow the valley,
click in the bones of willow,
snag in crab grass nesting in the dirt.

A crow is locked in the ice of heaven.

The river wants breaking.

Winter of the Dog,
Winter of the Wolf's Tooth,
Winter of the Chase.

I need your spring now, need

that country of affection:
green moons rising through a twilight
warm as skins, the tawny eucalyptus
stripped of bark, its whispered smells,
the fly-worms burning in the leaves.

# This Scrying

"Thus the conditions under which the scryer
can scry are, as yet, unascertained."
—Andrew Lang

Pausing by the sink, half stooped,
I study tea leaves emptied in a drain,
the sawdust sweetness of the pulp,
the pattern of my life to come
spread out before me like a map
in darkness I cannot cut through.
I run the tap, seeing how
the conditions will elude me further,
though I stare through centuries,
blinking into spheres, or hold
my palm out, tracing
my affections in a scrawl of lines.
And whether I shall have you here
beside me for another night
I will learn by reading closely
from your lips, but you
say nothing. It would seem,
the conditions against this scrying
are a bold prevention figured in the stars.

# To His Dear Friend, Bones

The arguments against restraint
in love, in retrospect, seem quaint;
I would have thought this obvious
to you, at least, whose serious
pursuit of intellectual grace
is not less equal to your taste
for all things richly formed. No good
will come of what we force. I should
be hesitant to say how long
this shy devotion has gone on,
how days beyond account have turned
to seasons as we've slowly learned
to speak a common tongue, to find
the world's erratic text defined
and stabilized. I should be vexed
to mention time at all, except
that, even as I write, a blear
October dampness feels like fear
externalized; I number days
in lots of thirty—all the ways
we have for counting breaths, so brief,
beside the measures of our grief
and joy. So let me obviate
this cold chronology and state
more simply what I mean: it's sure
enough, the grave will make obscure
whatever fierce, light moments love
affords. I should not have to prove
by metaphysical displays
of wit how numerous are the ways
in which it matters that we touch,
not merely with our hearts; so much
depends upon the skin, dear bones,
with all its various, humid tones,
the only barrier which contrives
to keep us in our separate lives.

# Sleepers

When in the course of sleep you turn and touch
my shoulder, hanging on to me as if
the scalloped ocean of your dreams were much
too much to bear alone, I know the reft
that forms between true lovers when they sleep
is partial, almost something to be wished
were it not there. And when from that same deep
a garbled syllable of fear is fished
and tossed between us on the waking deck
with cool and jeweled eyes, I wait to see
if sleep won't come again to haul it back
beneath those waters. Huddled in the lee
of our affection, we can well afford
cold creatures, distances, the alien word.

# Her Sadness

He held her. She was sad.
And nothing could disguise
the mist upon her eyes.
Yet every way he spoke
seemed only to evince
the sense that something bad
had happened in her night.
The room was full of light;
it settled on the flowers
beside their bed, the sheets
illumined by the sun.
He knew of all the powers
beyond what he could see:
the current of her dreams
wherein she had been whirled,
for hours tossed and churned.
"I love you," he might say,
but she would turn aside
and bite her lip to chide;
the most he could provide
was skin against her skin
and silence like the moss
that covers with green fur
the sharpest, rasping ledge
in time. She wept alone,
an island in the creek
of all his running love.
By noon, when they had slept
an hour past her tears,
they went outside. Her fears
had blown off like a fog
from that disconsolate shore.
They walked, now hand in hand,
and nothing more was said.
It was as if the dead
had somehow been subdued,
at least until that dark
came down on her again.

# After the Summer Heroes

*for D.S.J.*

After the summer heroes dwindle into names
on dusty gum-cards stacked in boxes
buried in the rooms we never search;

after all the Cokes, the candied apples,
cigarettes and beer consumed in haste,
converting into flesh and world to burn;

after all the sweethearts run amok
in cheap motel rooms, giving in to fear
that no one in the end will grant them time

to prosper or endure, time out to waste
in painted nails and factories of hair,
in drive-ins or the harping wards of babes;

after every dream of glory or of grace
in smooth performance of the given task
is punctured by the dismal needle, time—

love, may we catch some fragment of a song,
a canticle of blessed and bitter hours,
a lost refrain to carry into night.

# The Hawk of Love

*for Dorrie and Paul on Their Wedding*

Taloned,
with its horny beak and sootfall wings,
the hawk is high there,
flying in the dawn before we breathe.

Its eye is spectral, honing on the world,
a field of vision widening with height.

The wet ravines cannot evade it,
nor the mouths of caves.
Those hiding among tares will not be saved.

The lone eye searches from the pink of dawn
to wine-deep dusk. And even
in the dark its lunar pupil
widens as it burns, a treetop vigil,
nightly in its nest of beak and claws.

The green globe, spinning
through a blue and changeless heaven,
holds its prey. The wind wires
steady with their high-pitched humming
one hawk's stare.

Its swoop is glory, terrible and sure.
The cycles of the green earth yield to blue.
Its beak is bloody, but it makes us new.

# This Reaping

# This Reaping

They are all going out around us,
popping off like lights—
the professors crumpled over desks,
the doctors with entrails hanging from their ears,
the operators dead at the end of lines.

They are all going out, shut off
at the source without warning—
the student tumbled from a bike in traffic,
the child in its cradle, choking,
the nun in a faulty subway.

And nobody knows the hour,
whether now or later, whether
neatly with a snap in the night
or, less discreetly, dragged
by a bus through busy corners.

What a business, this reaping
in private or public places
with so little sowing:
let us pray that somewhere
on sweaty beds of complete affection
there are lovers
doubling themselves in the lively dark.

# Skater in Blue

The lid broke, and suddenly the child
in all her innocence was underneath
the ice in zero water, growing wild
with numbness and with fear. The child fell
so gently through the ice that none could tell
at first that she was gone. They skated on
without the backward looks that might have saved
her when she slipped, feet first, beneath the glaze.
She saw the sun distorted by the haze
of river ice, a splay of light, a lost
imperfect kingdom. Fallen out of sight,
she found a blue and simple, solid night.
It never came to her that no one knew
how far from them she'd fallen or how blue
her world had grown so quickly, at such cost.

# The Hunters

If you wait by a lick, they will find you,
the hunters, fathers and sons,
with hard blue fingers dragging the ground,
their scarlet jackets bleeding in the wind
as they wade through fields.

So many of them, pushing through burdock,
foraging, stepping over branches.
They have learned to come noiselessly,
shielding their grins; they will crouch
forever in the rain, upwind.

There is no use hiding, so let them
find you, flick their triggers
and bring you down.
So let them believe it matters, that
your body is more of you than the wind.

# Summer People

See them, the affectionate ones,
how they dawdle in the sun on watered lawns,
how they cast one shadow and call it love.

See the husbands playing at tennis,
shouting the scores, their smooth limbs
perfect in all proportions,

bobbing and weaving, winning or losing
weight and wives. Some knees are
bandaged to support their passion.

It is so important, they say,
knowing how to serve, not balking
when you swing, staying close to the line.

See the slender ladies with children
who look like themselves; they have married
these men with long vacations,

these summery people who know how
to do it, year after year,
how to find the time, the beautiful

houses on winking lakes, the friends
with even more luck than themselves,
the words to endear them each to another.

# Talking Transatlantic

*for Tony Ashe*

We should not be allowed to do this.

In the days when talk was cheap
and purely local,
we would send our messages by post,
black ink and blotters
plotting to dissuade, to comfort or cajole.

My lies were elegantly decked in truth.
My truths were bald, defiant fiction.

Time could save us from the quick response—
the time of letters digging in the page;
the time of paper, envelopes and stamps
all marshaled to conduct us to our ends.

But now we dial to exchange our lives.
The bedded wires shudder under seas
cold fathoms deep
to bear our meanings, trivial or grave.

My lies have lost their way of coming true.
My truths are nothing that the wind won't wear.

# Ice Fishing

The snow ticks off my cheeks, I raise my eyes,
and flakes like houseflies buzz against my gaze.
The ice squeaks underfoot as I go out
to fish on Hatchet Pond through frozen gauze.

The day whites out whichever way I look.
Big hemlocks ring the pond, their branches light
as dove wings, drooping feathers to the ground.
The blank eye hates this poverty of sight

and digs. I chip away the month of freeze
and splinter with an ax the ice that grows
like cancer inward from a whitish skin.
The minnows fly like sparks beneath my blows.

The taphole plunges like a wrist through ice,
then water breaks in ringlets of blue frost.
I drop a line along it back to summer,
fishing inside myself for what I've lost.

# Black Week

I must parse the sentence of my sadness,
diagram despair.
I must break my anger into parts of speech:
the nouns of nothing I can do or say,
the verbs of ruin, participles
raging through my fevered nights.
I must find a stronger subject for my verbs,
disrupt the syntax of protracted fear.
I must place my anger in subordination,
possess the grammar of my own recovery,
find my predicate, someone gladly
to complete my transitive, hungry verbs.

# Illimitable Kingdom

There is something about this room
you cannot pretend to say.
I stand by the window
where a green plane rises over towers.
It is full of silence, lifting
its nose into brilliant spaces.
Taxis throttle in the streets below,
but the room holds still;
the furniture waits at my convenience.

When the telephone rings, I let it
tremble and refuse to answer.
I cannot say why.
Alone in this wordless room,
I am grateful for the life
that will not give in, that keeps
on coming when the words are gone,
this world within world,
illimitable kingdom.

# Blue Day

Beginning without shadows,
softly, without sun: it starts
in night-blue filaments, in beams
extracted from the eye of darkness,
wound to light.
                    A blue beginning
in the space that falls between us
in our sleep, a sleight of air,
the thread of waking
pulled and spooled.
                    We sit
together in the bed sheets, naked,
failing to decide if we have slept,
or if, still dreaming,
we have met as shades to walk the world.

The dawn resists our concentration.
Blue, these walls. Blue pallor
of our skin, blue lawns outside.

The hour is a globe, revolving, still,
the noon of nothing. Zero
is the sum.
                    We make
no shadows on the ground we pass,
as if two ghosts glide quietly above
the flat, blue world.
                    My breath
is blue. Your fingers
chill the parchment of my skin.

# Naming the Losses

*for Luke, killed in Montana*

The floorboards sobbing overhead, my eighty-year-old
neighbor is awake at 3 A.M.
and listing through the dark.
He hunches by the sink
and spews sour phlegm.
Pain rings in the plumbing
like a tooth gone bad.
No way to sleep now, lying
naked, sweating in my sheets,
I leaf through pictures
of another life, of dark-eyed
Sarah and her love. It's
late for going into town
or taking showers or driving
into mountains where
the spruce and tamarack
keep a silence we cannot
maintain.
        I was eating
breakfast when I heard
you crashed, your light plane
flipping as it landed:
wisps of fire, wings
crumpled in the dirt.
You died at twenty, flying
to the West. I'm thirty,
but it feels far off,
this dying, farther off
than sleep.
        I met you
mornings in my class on Milton.
Green-eyed, a rebel,
you'd have fought with heaven
for the right to rule a kingdom
of your own, you told us,
grinning as the class demurred.

The Christians hastened
to assail your pride.

You came to see me
One night after dinner, sad,
reluctant to betray your feelings.
But I fed you whiskey
till you said the only woman
you had ever loved was going
West, she needed time,
you didn't know for what.
I told you it was time
you had to give, holding
your shoulders firmly
in my hands.
          My lame words
stagger in the path of sorrows.
Pictures wrinkle in my palms,
all Sarah, hair across
her forehead like a crow's
black wing. The pulse
breaks softly underneath
my pillow; bloodwaves
shatter on the rocks,
hard hours. The old man's
dying in the drain upstairs.

Sweet Luke, believe me.
I will name you dearly
in the endless losses
I am always counting:
summer's generation dying
in the fall, the long night's
waking, elders stumbling
in their darkened rooms,
Sarah in the salt Pacific air.

# In the Wind

*at Boarhills, Fife*

════════

### 1

Here at Boarhills
the black rocks boom against the surf,
the waves beginning from a point far-off
and swelling to a crest
like vague nostalgia for a distant lover.
Silver rollers spill into the shore,
the shingle rasping,
salty grasses lathered by the spray.

Here, standing on the cliff,
we watch a red sun darkening the firth,
a solitary tern low over water,
slicing through the air with fiery wings.
As night hoods over:
shadows on the ground, a blue
crêpe nightdress on the bedroom floor.

We lean into the wind
as tides slip back, exposing
sea wrack, limpets on the rocks,
the skulls of herring. Ghost crabs
slither through the tang of kelp,
their slow invasion of the dimming land.
And mindlessly the darkest velvet evening
buries us alive.

### 2

We lie here in the whirling tent of night,
camping by the sea wall, listening
through the flaps to wind that drones.
You say you are afraid.
I ask you to be still and pull you tight.
The wax lamp gutters. Love
has drained like daylight from our bones.

### 3

I go down early to the sea alone
while you're asleep.

Gulls are mewing on a bank of water.
Out along the beachhead, almost to the point,
a glinting rockpool claims my vision.
In it lies the pulsing, iron heart
of Ocean under glass, a yellow coil,
anemone,
a pumping golden fist, the ventricles aflame.

If I should pluck it from its shining nest
of bladderwrack and kelp, the tides might stop.
The sun might hover in this spot forever.
Terns might dangle in the freeze of space,
wings made of sunlight,
cutting through the soft, eternal boom
of Ocean in its swell.

I wonder if your heart could thus
be drawn, be taken
from its nest of bone and gristle,
hidden from the world, held in these hands?

### 4

We listen to the harping, shapeless vowel
of wind across the water,
waiting at the bright
and bitter margin where the sea begins:
the ancient whale-road keening to the north,
the brindled main. The sun's
a brilliant tonnage in the blue, but
metaphor resists us, wind on sand;
the consonantal cliffs cannot
contain rude motions of the air.

A babble of debris drifts down the beach,
loose grass and cockles, cuttlebones
and branches. Black rocks

boom, and shingle in the surf is clean
and rasping. Gulls
go bleating overhead as if
they've got a message we must only hear.
The hieroglyphic clouds address the sky.

I take your hand, oh, trying to descry
the name of loss, the raw-wet language
drying into words not quite the same.

We hold and listen, needing
to be still, to gather witness,
wait on voices shunting in the wind.

# Near Aberdeen

"History broods over that part of the world
like the easterly haar."

—R. L. Stevenson

On a blue scarp, far out, musing
over water, standing where the salt winds
whet their blades on granite edges,
hogweeds rasping, marram grass and thistle,
I was north of Aberdeen,
alone and calling to a friend
as if the wind could carry to her heart
my words like spores, as if
by merely shouting in the air
past waters snarling in the rocks
affection could be raised, its sword
and fire, the blue flame
rising in the mist, the lifting haar.

# High Gannet

*for Robert Penn Warren*

I watch it breaking from a cliff,
a gannet with its white-silk wings,
chipped off, a piece of granite, swung out wide.

Through shelves of light it rises,
through the plum-ripe dawn,
its fringe of shadows, blood-bright clouds
accumulating orchids, froths of bloom.

Way up, it hangs an eye upon the world.

Cold sea bird, risen out of time
through mizzling fog to ice-blue air,
I know the journey you in flight describe:
from rock to water, water into fog,
from fog to sunlit drizzle into air—

to live forever in the air's idea,
mindless as a star,
a gannet in perpetual blue flight,
pure breath above the world.